ANNA'S RAIN

Story by Fred Burstein

Pictures by Harvey Stevenson

ORCHARD BOOKS / NEW YORK

Text copyright © 1990 by Fred Burstein. Illustrations copyright © 1990 by Harvey Stevenson.

Orchard Books, A division of Franklin Watts, Inc., 387 Park Avenue South, New York, NY 10016

Manufactured in the United States of America.   Printed by General Offset Co., Inc. Bound by Horowitz/Rae
The text of this book is set in 24 pt. ITC Eras Medium.
The illustrations are watercolors with pencil, reproduced in halftone.
Book design by Mina Greenstein. 10   9   8   7   6   5   4   3   2   1

Library of Congress Cataloging-in-Publication Data
Burstein, Fred.   Anna's rain / by Fred Burstein ; illustrated by Harvey Stevenson.   p.   cm.
"A Richard Jackson book"
Summary: Anna Lee and her father feed the birds on a rainy day.
ISBN 0-531-05827-1.   ISBN 0-531-08427-2 (lib. bdg.)
[1. Birds—Fiction.   2. Fathers and daughters—Fiction.]   I. Stevenson, Harvey, ill.   II. Title.
PZ7.B945534An   1989   [E]—dc20   89-42533   CIP   AC

For my parents,
Daniel and Judith—F.B.

To Grandma B.,
who loves to feed the birds—H.S.

"Anna Lee . . ."

"It's all right, Daddy. I'm not doing anything."

"Are you getting bird food all over the porch?"

"It's raining out, honey. You can't feed the birds now."

"Well, I have to."

"Birds don't even eat when it's raining. . . ."

"But they might get cold and starve, Daddy."

"Will you take the umbrella?"

"Sure, Daddy. Up!"

"You mean I have to go too?"

"Up!"

"Anna, listen. The rain is turning into ice."

"What? Are you kidding?"

"Stick your hand out and feel it."

"Can I pour the food in?"

"We made it!"

"I can't believe my eyes."

"Don't tell me there are birds there already!"

"That was close. They were sure hungry."

"One sounds like: Snow tonight, snow tonight."

"She's saying: Thank you, Anna."